P JO

The Witch's Children

Henry Holt and Company, LLC
Publishers since 1866
115 West 18th Street
New York, New York 10011
www.henryholt.com

Henry Holt is a registered trademark of
Henry Holt and Company, LLC
Text copyright © 2001 by Ursula Jones
Illustrations copyright © 2001 by Russell Ayto
First published in the United States in 2003 by Henry Holt and Company
Originally published in Great Britain in 2001 by Orchard Books

Library of Congress Cataloging-in-Publication Data
Jones, Ursula.
The witch's children / written by Ursula Jones; illustrated by Russell Ayto.
Summary: When the two older witch's children use their magic to create trouble in the
park, the Little One knows how to fix the problem.
[1. Witches—Fiction. 2. Magic—Fiction. 3. Parks—Fiction.] I. Ayto, Russell, ill. II. Title.
PZ7.J72755 Wi 2003   [E]—dc21   2002005943

ISBN 0-8050-7205-5 / First American Edition—2003
Printed in Hong Kong
1 3 5 7 9 10 8 6 4 2

The Witch's Children

written by

Ursula Jones

illustrated by

Russell Ayto

Henry Holt and Company • New York

For Charlotte
—U. J.

For Matthew and Daniel
—R. A.

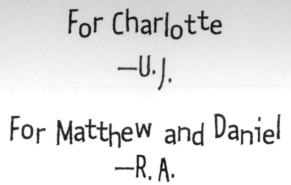

One windy day the witch's children
went to the park.

"Look out," said the pigeons.
"Here come the witch's children!"
And they flew into the trees.

"Look out," said the squirrels. "The witch's children are coming and that means TROUBLE!" And they ran up the tree trunks into the wind-tossed trees.

It was quite crowded up there.

The witch's children bought ice creams
from the ice-cream lady.
The Eldest and the Middle One bought two each.
The Little One bought three.

"So far, no trouble," said the pigeons to the squirrels.

The witch's children came to the pond.
Gemma was sailing her boat.

The wind blew

and blew.

*It blew the
boat over.*

"I will," said the Eldest One, and he changed Gemma . . .

. . . into . . .

. . . a frog.

"Swim out and rescue your boat," said the
Eldest One to the frog. So Gemma did.

"That was fun," said Gemma.
"Change me back now, please."
"Can't," said the Eldest One.
"I haven't learned how to do that yet."
The frog cried and cried.
"Now we've got trouble,"
cooed the pigeons.

And the Little One laughed until she fell over.

"Don't worry, Gemma," said the Middle One to the frog. "Watch."

She changed the trees into a huge palace.

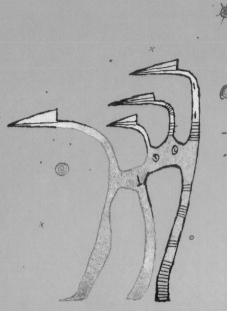

And the pigeons into fat footmen.

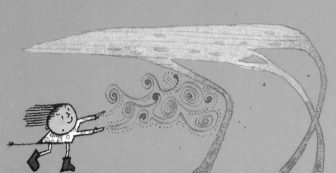

And the squirrels into smart soldiers.

She changed the ice-cream truck into a golden coach.

And the ice-cream lady into a fair princess.

"Kiss the frog," said the witch's child to the princess.

So the princess did.

And the frog turned
into a handsome prince.

"That's no good," said the prince.
"I want to be Gemma. Change us all back."

"Yes," snapped the princess. "This coach is full of melted ice cream. Change us back."

"Can't," said the Middle One. "I haven't learned how to do that yet."

"Now we're in trouble," sighed the footmen to the soldiers.

And the Little One laughed till she split her trousers.

"STOP THAT!"

they all shouted. "And get us out of trouble."
The Little One felt sorry she'd laughed at them.
"I only know one bit of magic."

"Well, try it!"

they all said.
   The Little One opened her mouth
wide and yelled . . .

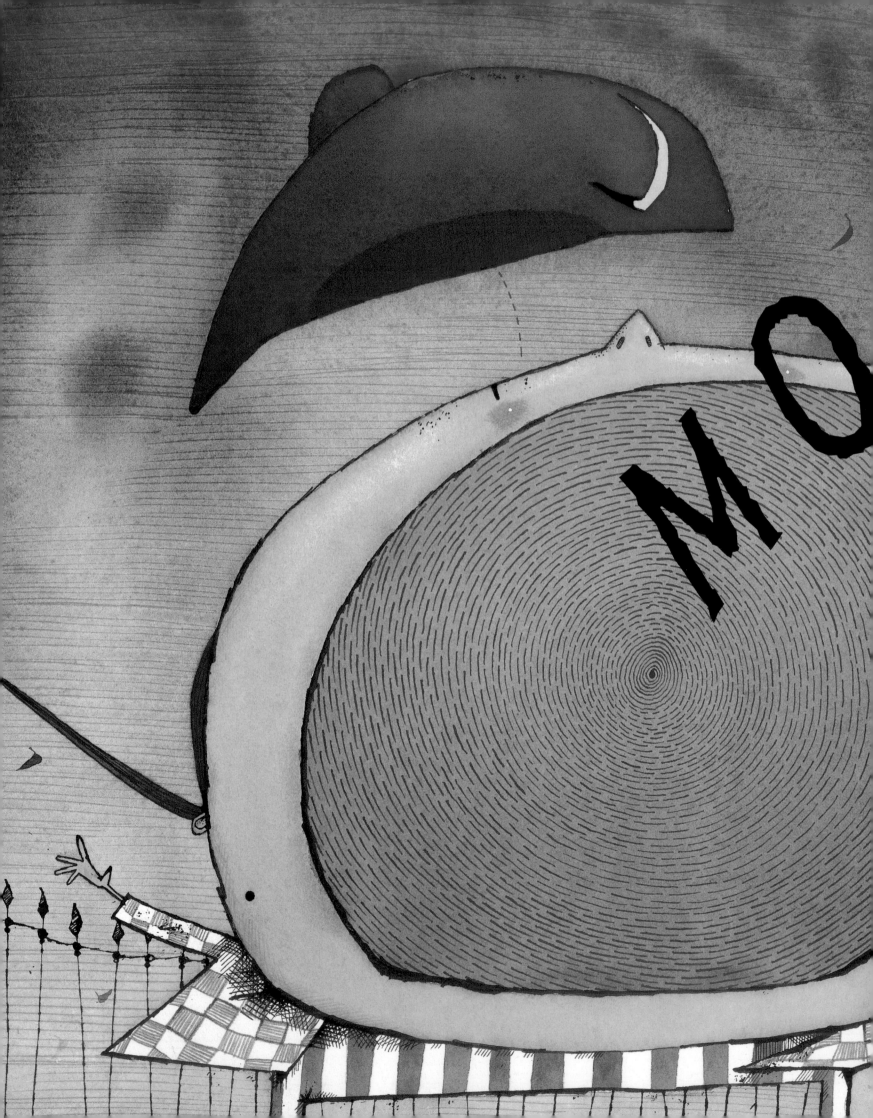

And . . .

WHOOSH!

...out of the clouds flew the witch on her broomstick.

She changed the handsome prince back into Gemma . . .

the fair princess back into the ice-cream lady . . .

the golden coach back into the ice-cream truck . . .

the smart soldiers back into the squirrels . . .

the fat footmen back into the pigeons . . .

and the huge palace back into the trees.

And they were all happy.

Especially the Little One.

And the witch's children flew home
on their mother's broomstick . . .

. . . and they all had cake.